THE
BIG GAME
FROM THE
BLACK LAGOON®

Get more monster-sized laughs from

The Black Lagoon®

THE
BIG GAME
FROM THE
BLACK LAGOON®

GOBBLE,
GOBBLE.

by Mike Thaler
Illustrated by Jared Lee

SCHOLASTIC INC.

To Alex and Betty Wagner:
Happy 70th Anniversary!—M.T.

To Junior, Skidmark, and Captain Jack—J.L.

ISBN 978-0-545-61639-3

Text copyright © 2013 by Mike Thaler
Illustrations copyright © 2013 by Jared D. Lee Studio, Inc.

12 11 10 9 8 7 6 5 4 3 2   13 14 15 16 17 18/0

Printed in the U.S.A.   40
First printing, November 2013

CONTENTS

CHAPTER 1

THE CHALLENGE

Next week is Thanksgiving. It's almost time for all the football bowl games.

There are lots of them:
The Orange Bowl.

← JUICY ORANGES

The Fiesta Bowl.

← SPICY HOT BURRITOS

The Pizza Bowl.

DOUBLE CHEESE
MEATBALL
PEPPERONI
PIZZA
ANCHOVY

The Rose Bowl, and more.

PINK ROSES
RED ROSES

The fourth-grade team has challenged us, the third-grade team, to a football game. They're bigger, stronger, and meaner than us.

SPIKE HAIR

FAKE TATTOO

GRRRR...

WOLF TEETH

FOURTH GRADER

THIRD GRADER

9

It'll be "The Toilet Bowl." Eric says they're not smarter, they're just bullies. Maybe we should call the game "The Bully Bowl."

Mrs. Green says we should call
it "The Turkey Bowl."
Eric says we should call it that
because they're such big turkeys.

Mrs. Green is our coach. This should be good!

WHICH BALL DO WE USE?

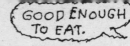

CHAPTER 2

BY ANY OTHER NAME

After school, we have our first team meeting. The whole class is there, even the girls. They want to play. Mrs. Green says they can.

← SPEED BUG

Mrs. Green says we need a team name. The boys suggest the Lions, the Tigers, and the Pit Bulls. The girls suggest the Puppies, the Kittens, and the Teddy Bears.

I don't see how this is going to work out at all. Mrs. Green says we should compromise, so we finally decide on the Cool Cats.

CHAPTER 3
MUDDLE IN THE HUDDLE

Next, we need to choose our positions. There's *quarterback*, *halfback*, *tailback*, and *fullback*.

PENNY, THERE'S NO SUCH THING AS A PENNYBACK.

Eric says we should be *left back*.
Next, there's the ends.
There's the *tight end* (that's definitely Randy), and the *wide end* (that's Freddy).

Penny and Doris want to be on the line. They think it's a chorus line so they can dance. I'd like to be safety so I won't get hurt.

18

Next Mrs. Green says we need plays. Penny suggests *Romeo and Juliet.*

This is going to be horrible. The fourth grade is going to flatten us. We'll be bowled over.

← BOWLING BALL

CHAPTER 4

NEVER GIVE UP

When I get home, I tell Mom about the game. She tells me to sit down and she gives me a glass of milk and a chocolate-chip cookie.

"Hubie, have you ever heard of David and Goliath?"

"No, Mom. Who did they play for?"

"They lived a long time ago. David was a small shepherd boy and Goliath was a fifteen-foot bully."

← SHEEP

21

"He would have been a good linebacker. He could have played for the Giants."

"He *was* a giant and David had to fight him."

"Like us and the fourth grade?"

"Like you and the fourth grade."

"Was he scared, Mom?" I ask.

"Sure he was scared. But it didn't stop him from standing up to the giant."

"What happened, Mom?"

"Well, David stood up, stayed up, and won."

"Maybe we can win, too, Mom."

"You won't know until you try, Hubie."

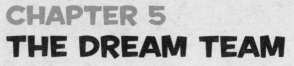

CHAPTER 5
THE DREAM TEAM

That night I had a dream. I was playing in the Super Bowl. We were playing the Giants, and they were *real* giants. I was playing every position. I was the whole team and we were losing.

WAKE UP! IT'S TIME FOR ME TO CHASE YOU.

There was a minute left in the game and the score was 128 to 0. Mrs. Green was the coach and Mom was the cheerleader. I had the ball on my own five-yard line.

"Don't give up, Hubie!" cheered my mom.

REALLY, MOM?

I DON'T WANT TO BE IN THIS DREAM.

I hiked the ball to myself and followed my blocker, which was also me. I ran through a giant's legs. Then I spun and shot down the sideline. Everyone was cheering—no one could catch me. They were big, but they were slow. I shot into the end zone. Touchdown!

The score was 128 to 6 and the game ended.

I was voted MVP and believe it or not, my team won. Hey, it's my dream, and when you dream—anything's possible.

CHAPTER 6
PRACTICE MAKES PERFECT

The next day in art class, we tie-dyed our team T-shirts. They were rainbow-colored and said "Cool Cats" on the front. We *were* cool cats.

After school, we had our first practice. It didn't go so good. Doris, who was center, rolled the ball back to Eric, who was quarterback. He picked it up and threw it to Randy, who dropped it.

33

Freddy fell on the ball, which bounced out to Derek, who kicked it to me. I caught it and got turned around and ran the

wrong way. It was a touchdown—
but for the other team. Oh, well.
Nobody's perfect.

CHAPTER 7
HOW YOU PLAY THE GAME

The next day in the library, I checked out all the books about football. There were some about great players who overcame obstacles. They just wouldn't give up. I don't know if they'll ever write a book about me—I'm almost ready to give up now.

FOURTH GRADER   FIFTH GRADER

Why doesn't the fourth grade play the fifth grade instead? Then we could play the second grade. We'd be bigger, stronger, and . . . bullies. Wait a minute, that's

38

THIRD GRADER   SECOND GRADER

not right. I guess it's just as it should be. I don't want to be a bully, I'd rather be a hero. Maybe our team name should be the Underdogs.

CHAPTER 8
THE THUNDER DOGS!

Tomorrow after school is game day. The cafeteria table has become our training table. Today, Freddy had four desserts and our wide end is becoming wider. The fourth graders sit at the next table and talk trash for the whole period.

THAT'S CUTE. NOW CAN I HAVE MY HAT BACK?

"Hey, wimps, eat now because tomorrow you'll *be* lunch."

"I hope your disaster insurance is paid up."

"I'm bringing a calculator to add up our score."

And just as we're leaving, they sneer, "Good-bye, chickens, see you tomorrow."

PECK.
PECK.
PECK.

I turn to them, look them in the eyes, and say, "Don't count your chickens until they hatch."

Outside of the cafeteria my knees are shaking.

"What did that mean, anyway?" asks Eric.

"Beats me," I answer.

⟵ CHICKEN

CHAPTER 9
GOING DOWN THE TUBE

It's my last night to prepare and there's a game on TV. Actually, there's a game on TV almost every night of the week. Everyone loves football. Mrs. Beamster says it's just like the Romans. They all went to the Coliseum to watch the lions play on Sunday.

THE
LIBRARIAN →

I watch the game and pretend I'm the running back—I cut right, I cut left, I spin, I'm dizzy, I run the wrong way—for a touchdown— too bad it's for the other team.

Hey, if I keep running the wrong way, I could set an NFL record—most touchdowns for the other team. I'd give *running back* a whole new meaning.

CHAPTER 10
GAME DAY

GO, GIANTS!

Well, the big day has arrived. GAME DAY! The whole school has come to watch. The bleachers are full. All the girls in the fourth

OH, GREAT.

grade are cheerleaders. Our girls
are playing. We all put on our
team T-shirts and run onto the
field.

The fourth grade has T-shirts, too. They're black and say "Giants." They don't have to rub it in.

Our rainbow uniforms are prettier.

We kick off and they run it back for a touchdown. Hey, that was fast.

They kick off to us and we go three and out. In other words, we go nowhere.

They get the ball back and score another touchdown. This is getting boring. At halftime, we're losing 70 to 0.

Mrs. Green gives a great halftime pep talk. She says our T-shirts are nicer and we only have another half to go. Well, the second half goes pretty much like the first. There's one minute left and the score is 140 to 0.

It's time for a last-minute rally.

CHAPTER 11
ZERO TO HERO

They kick off and I catch it on my own five-yard line.

Hey, I've been here before—just like my dream. I tuck the ball under my arm and start upfield. I cut right, I cut left. . . .

I duck, I spin, I hurdle, I twirl,
I'm unstoppable . . . I SCORE!
Touchdown, third grade!

HE RUNS LIKE A RABBIT!

HE SLIPPED RIGHT THROUGH MY HANDS.

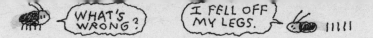

I look around. I hope I'm in the right end zone. I am! My team runs up and gives me high fives and hugs. Even the girls—ech! We all cheer as the points go up on the scoreboard. 140–6. Hey, it's a start! Wait till next year.

Even the fourth graders come over and congratulate me on my run. My team votes me MVP and they give me the game ball. I'm already beginning to feel bigger and stronger.

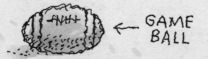

← GAME BALL

CHAPTER 12
CELEBRATION

Mrs. Green takes us all to Pizza Mutt for our celebration dinner. We order the giant combo pizza with everything on it . . . except anchovies. While we're waiting for it, we all tell our favorite stories about the game and we make up special awards for everyone on the team.

Freddy gets the widest end award.

Eric gets the funniest joke award—which was: "How'd Hubie make a touchdown? Because his nose was running."

Penny gets the most polite player award and Doris gets the cleanest T-shirt award.

When the pizza comes, we all give our team cheer, which I make up between bites:

Cool cats,
You're the best forever more
Don't even worry about the score
As long as we arrived and tried
Our faces we don't have to hide
So give yourselves a mighty
 cheer
And look forward to more
 games next year.

NEXT DAY AT SCHOOL
HUBIE, YOU WANT TO SIT WITH ME DURING LUNCH?
HUBIE, CAN I HAVE YOUR AUTOGRAPH?
CAN I BE YOUR AGENT?
CLAP! CLAP!
MAKE WAY!
WILL YOU BE GOING PRO?